Star Girl is first published in the United States in 2015
by Picture Window Books
A Capstone imprint
1710 Roe Crest Drive
North Mankato, Minnesota 56003
www.capstonepub.com

Library of Congress Cataloging-in-Publication Data is available on the Library of
Congress website.

ISBN: 978-1-4795-8275-4 (library binding)
ISBN: 978-1-4795-8279-2 (paperback)
ISBN: 978-1-4795-8471-0 (eBook PDF)

Summary: Planet Polare's ice is melting, and now the alien life forms are in danger.
When Star Girl is sent to investigate with her roommate, she discovers that not all
dangers come from hairy aliens or strange planets. Can the two space cadets put aside
their differences and work together to save the planet and its inhabitants?

Designer: Natascha Lenz

This *New Girl* US Edition is published by arrangement with Macmillan Education
Australia Pty Ltd, 15 - 19 Claremont Street, South Yarra, Vic 3141, Australia

Printed in the United States of America by Corporate Graphics

STAR ★ GIRL

SAVING SPACE ONE PLANET AT A TIME

NEW GIRL

LOUISE PARK

PICTURE WINDOW BOOKS
a capstone imprint

SPACE EDUCATION

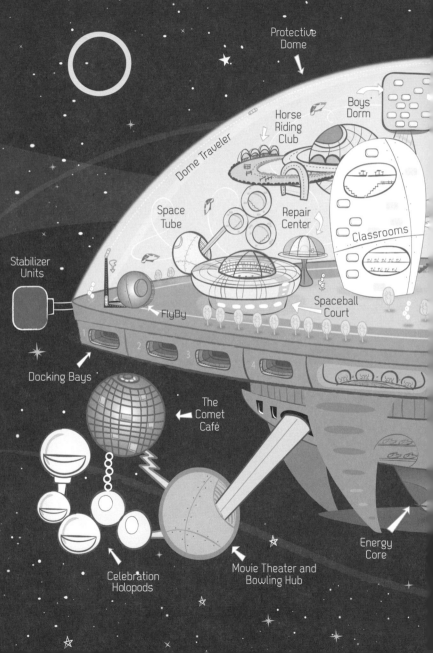

Protective Dome

Boys' Dorm

Horse Riding Club

Dome Traveler

Space Tube

Repair Center

Classrooms

Stabilizer Units

Spaceball Court

FlyBy

Docking Bays

The Comet Café

Celebration Holopods

Movie Theater and Bowling Hub

Energy Core

AND ACTION SCHOOL

Staff Only Zone

Staff Quarters

Space Tube

Girls' Dorm

Gymnasium and Ballet Studio

Classrooms

Agricultural Center

Space Flight Training Center

Docking Bays

Escape Pod

Beach Island

SEAS

A SPACE STATION BOARDING SCHOOL FOR GIRLS AND BOYS

The Space Education and Action School (SEAS) is located on Space Station Edumax. Students in the space training program complete space missions on planets in outer space that are in danger and need help.

Not all students will make it through to their final year and only the best students will go on to become space agents. Addie must make it through and become a Space Agent. Outer space needs her.

Program: Space Cadetship

Student: Adelaide Banks

Space Cadet: Star Girl

Age: 10 years old

School house: Stellar

Space missions: 0

Earned mission points: 0

Earned house points: 0

Comments: Adelaide's entrance exam scores were not high enough to earn her a place in the Space Cadet program's first round. Joining the program late in the term has made it difficult for Adelaide and she will have to work hard to keep up.

CHAPTER ★ ONE

STAR GIRL TO JESS

5 things you need to know about Valentina:

1. She can't stand messes. The room has to be like really perfect.
2. She doesn't think I should be here.
3. She thinks she's the best. So what if she's the highest-scoring space cadet?
4. She doesn't like me.
5. It's like she rules everyone and everything.

Addie 😦

JESS TO STAR GIRL

Yuck! Tidy kinda isn't your thing, Ads! You need a new roomie. Can you get one?

Jess 🧸

Addie smiled. Jess's little bear hugs always made her feel better.

Addie was in her dorm room. It was Monday afternoon. She was sending messages to her friends back home on Earth. Addie was using her SpaceBerry. It was a small computer and a cell phone. All the space cadets were given one when they started at SEAS.

SCHOOL ISSUE SPACEBERRY

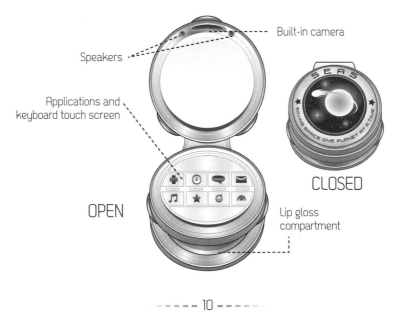

Built-in camera

Speakers

Applications and keyboard touch screen

OPEN

SEAS
SAVING SPACE ONE PLANET AT A TIME

CLOSED

Lip gloss compartment

Addie loved her SpaceBerry. She'd never had a cell phone before. *I just wish I had someone I could call on it here*, thought Addie. It was okay to send messages back home, but phone calls cost too much money. And she didn't have any real friends at SEAS yet. She'd only been there three weeks.

Addie was just about to write back to Jess when Valentina burst through the dorm room door. "Sending messages to your silly little friends again, Adelaide? Let me guess—writing to Paris?" Valentina said with a mean little laugh. "You'll be home soon anyway, I'm sure. You didn't really make it into SEAS. We all know you're only here because someone else left."

Addie snapped her SpaceBerry shut. She thought about saying something back. Something like how she'd made it in because she was at the top of the list and next in line for a spot. But she didn't. *Maybe if I just ignore her she'll go away*, thought Addie.

"And do something with those gross pajamas. Eeew!" said Valentina.

"They're on the floor on my side of the room. Not yours," said Addie.

"I don't care," said Valentina. "My room. My rules."

"Actually, it's our room," Addie mumbled. *But you'd never know it*, she added silently. Valentina's gymnastics trophies and awards from her old school took up almost every shelf.

Now I know why the last roommate thought boarding school wasn't for her, thought Addie. *But I plan on staying no matter what.*

Addie pushed her pajamas into the Press and Pick. The P&P had a chute for dirty clothes and a hanging space for clean clothes. Its touch screen had a picture of every piece of clothing that was put into it. Addie just picked the clothes she wanted on the touch screen. In no time the clothes were floating in the hanging space, all clean and pressed. It was so efficient, although sometimes it did have little wardrobe malfunctions. One time Addie got her school blazer and a bikini top.

Addie closed the lid on the P&P. Then she turned and looked at Valentina. She was picking up Addie's stuffed animals one by one from Addie's bed.

Addie's tummy started doing backflips.

"And stick these stupid things in there too," Valentina said. "Or I'll make sure they don't come back."

Addie grabbed her penguin before Valentina got to it. She'd had it since she was little, and she loved it to death. "I can have whatever I want on my bed."

"They're dirty and messy looking," said Valentina. "I don't want them in the room."

Addie knew her animals weren't safe from Valentina. She was looking for a safe place to lock them away when the big plasma screen on their bedroom wall flashed.

ALL STUDENTS TO THE
DINING HALL FOR DINNER

Good, thought Addie. She waited for

Valentina to go. Then she put her soft furry

friends in the drawer underneath her bed and

activated the lock.

* * * * *

Addie raced into the dining hall. She was a

little late, and everyone was already sitting

down at the tables. Addie looked around.

There was a spare seat next to Valentina and

her group. *I'm not going there,* thought Addie.

Then she saw Miyako and Olivia, the girls she'd been sitting with in Alien ID class. They were waving, and they'd saved her a seat.

Yes! thought Addie, and she raced over and sat down.

"So, how's Miss Valentina-mean-a today?" Olivia asked.

"She hates me," Addie said.

"She doesn't really hate you," Miyako said.

"What's with her anyway?" Addie was trying hard not to get angry, but she couldn't help it. "I asked to change rooms. But the dorm teacher, Mrs. Lamrock, said both Valentina and I have to agree for me to move. And Valentina said no! Why? She hates sharing her room with me. I thought she'd be happy to get rid of me."

"She'll never agree to a room change now," Olivia said. "Not when that she knows that's what you want. That's how she works."

Addie felt like she was about to cry.

"Come on, forget about her and let's eat," said Olivia.

The girls ate quietly for a while and then Miyako said, "Addie, you know Valentina just *wants* to make you sad, don't you?"

"I know," said Addie. "And she's doing a good job, too!"

"So, hang with us and be happy!" said Olivia. "It will drive her nuts."

Addie looked at Miyako and Olivia.

They were both making really silly happy faces at her. She burst out laughing. It was the first time she'd laughed all day. Then she made her eyes pop and pulled her mouth into a silly banana shape.

"You look good that way!" Olivia said, giggling.

"See!" Miya said. "Come on, there's apple pie and ice cream for dessert."

But just then Addie's SpaceBerry rang.

Ding Dong

Ding Dong

Addie had a doorbell sound for incoming messages on her SpaceBerry. It reminded her of home. "I'm wanted in the FlyBy," Addie said. "My first space mission! Awesome! Gotta go."

"Addie," Miya called after her, "have fun!"

"Thanks," Addie called back as she headed for the FlyBy. Her two friends were still making funny happy faces at her.

Addie smiled. *Who cares about Valentina?* she thought.

CHAPTER ★ TWO

Addie knew where the FlyBy was. She landed there in the school space shuttle a few weeks ago. But today it looked different. It was busy. There were stacks of landing bays and lots of SEAS space bots unloading food and supplies from all the space pods that had just landed. *This place is totally amazing,* thought Addie. *I love it!*

Addie found the mission briefing room, but the door was shut. She stood in front of the Face Scan screen on the door.

The screen beeped and then flashed.

BEEP BEEP

Addie opened the door and went inside.

"Oh great," Valentina groaned. "The new girl. I guess we'll be getting zero points for this mission."

Addie's mouth dropped open. Valentina was the last person she expected to see.

"Valentina!" said Mr. Cruise. "It's your job to help Adelaide on her first mission. And as always, you must work together. As a team."

Addie didn't look at Valentina. She stared at the floor. She hated being the new girl, and she didn't really like being called Adelaide.

"Okay, girls," said Mr. Cruise. "This mission is to the Halifax Galaxy. You'll be going to a planet there called Polare. It's an icy planet with lots of ice mountains, packed ice, and freezing seas. Something is melting the ice there. Your mission is to find out what."

"What space shuttle will we be going in?" asked Valentina.

"*Galactic Racer 2*," said Mr. Cruise. "We need to get you there as fast as possible.

The *Racer* has a small space pod on board. You'll use it to land on the planet. Can I have your watches, please? I need to upload myself as the mission holograph teacher. I'll also check to make sure that your chips are working."

GALACTIC RACER 2

Fuel tanks

Pod storage bay

Propulsion rockets

Pilot cockpit

GR2★

Luxury passenger cabin

Every cadet had a SEAS holographic watch that had to be worn at all times. Space cadets used them on missions to talk with their mission teacher. All a space cadet had to do was flip open the watch cover and the teacher was there, ready to help.

SCHOOL ISSUE HOLOGRAPHIC WATCH

Holographic communication activator

Volume and holograph controls

Speaker

5:30

GPS tracking chip

Teachers used the GPS tracking chip in the watches to keep track of their cadets on missions. They could find them anywhere, anytime using the tracking chip.

"I'll have everything ready for takeoff in about ten minutes," said Mr. Cruise. "Use the time to learn as much as you can about Planet Polare and its alien life forms."

The girls sat down at the FlyBy computers. Addie took out her SpaceBerry and plugged it into the computer. *I'll download some stuff onto my SpaceBerry*, she thought.

After she downloaded a photo of the aliens, she got up to go to the bathroom. On the way she took a look at Valentina's computer screen.

She's online chatting with friends! She hasn't done any work for the mission at all.

"Your watches are ready," said Mr. Cruise. "I'll check your spacesuits now."

"Thanks, Mr. Cruise," Valentina said.

Valentina waited until Mr. Cruise had turned away to look at the suits. Then she grabbed both watches. She quietly removed the chip from Addie's watch, then turned it off and slipped the chip into her shirt pocket. *That will get her into tons of trouble back at school*, Valentina thought.

A moment later, Addie came back into the room.

"The spacesuits are ready," said Mr. Cruise. "Hurry girls, gear up."

Addie looked at the spacesuits. They were all white with matching helmets, and they were kind of a weird shape.

The bottom looked super enormous. Addie pulled hers on and laughed.

"I'm not wearing that," said Valentina. "Where are the normal suits, Mr. Cruise?"

"These are normal suits, Supernova 1," Mr. Cruise answered. "We've just given you extra padding in the bottom, knees, and elbows. It's not a fashion show. The ice on Polare is very hard."

Mr. Cruise continued, "Now, we also have some new space boots for you. They have a few features on them for various environments. There are different soles for different surfaces.

You'll be needing the ice holds on your boots in Polare. The buttons for your boots are on your ice poles." Mr. Cruise picked up a set of poles. "These poles have special grips. The right grip has buttons to control your boots. The left grip has buttons for the base of the poles. There are two settings. Spike and shovel.

SPACE BOOTS AND POLES

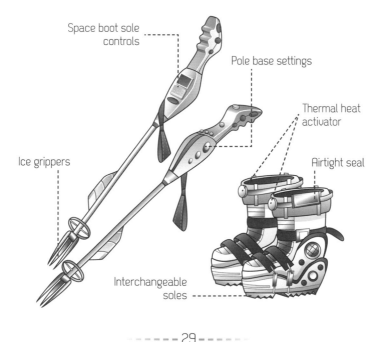

Space boot sole controls

Pole base settings

Thermal heat activator

Ice grippers

Airtight seal

Interchangeable soles

Shovel is handy when you need to dig through the snow."

Mr. Cruise took out his SpaceBerry and keyed in a code. The wall of the briefing room slid open. On the other side sat *Galactic Racer 2*.

"Your mission packs are waiting for you aboard the shuttle," said Mr. Cruise. "And you know the rules: Work as a team. Stay together at all times. Investigate and report back. Good luck, girls, and don't forget to call me if there's anything you need."

The girls climbed aboard. The hatch closed and Mr. Cruise was gone.

CHAPTER ★ THREE

Addie sat in her seat on *Galactic Racer 2*. As she did, air whooshed out from her spacesuit.

POOOF!

Valentina pulled her suit on and zipped it up. "I look ridiculous," she said. "I'll be surprised if I fit in the seat." She sat down beside Addie and a huge whoosh of air exploded into the cabin.

POOOOOOOF!

"Better than a whoopee cushion!" Addie laughed.

"Well, at least we're comfy," said Valentina with a giggle.

She looks pretty nice when she smiles, thought Addie. *It's good to be having some fun with her.*

Addie looked around the cabin. A big screen was mounted on the cockpit wall in front of them. There were handsets, headsets, and all kinds of gadgets and gizmos.

"Do we always get to fly in things as awesome as this?" Addie asked. "And where's the pod thing?"

A voice came through the cabin speakers. "So many questions, Star Girl," said the pilot.

"And hello again, Supernova 1. I'm Space Agent Space Surfer, and I'm your pilot on this mission. The pod is in the launching bay and yes, when I fly, we always fly in style!"

"Oh my gosh!" gasped Valentina. "It's Space Surfer. Awesome!"

"Who's Space Surfer?" asked Addie.

"Only the hottest learner pilot at our school," said Valentina.

"Learner pilot!" Addie repeated. She could feel those tummy backflips starting up again. "You mean he's learning to fly and flying us? Like, using us as practice?"

"Don't you know anything, new girl?" said Valentina. "First years are cadets. Second year we learn to fly. Third year we get to fly solo if we pass our tests."

"So, he can fly? He knows what he's doing?" Addie asked.

"Of course I know what I'm doing," said Space Surfer. Addie blushed. She didn't realize he could hear her. "I'm in my third year and I've passed all my tests. Please don't leave your seats during the flight. We'll be taking a few shortcuts to get you to the Halifax galaxy faster. Things might get a little bumpy. Just sit back and go with the flow."

"Don't worry," said Addie with a grin. "Our spacesuits have tons of extra padding. We'll be all right!"

"There's no way he's going to be seeing me in this stupid get-up," mumbled Valentina.

She turned on the in-flight theater on and begin watching a movie.

Addie looked out the cabin window. She couldn't stop looking at the thousands of different-colored stars. "It's amazing out there," she said. "I didn't know space was so colorful!" They flew past gas clouds and tons of other galaxies that looked like swirls of stardust. "I love space!" she said.

Just then the *Racer* rocked to the left. Then it rocked to the right. The girls had to hold on to their seats. The *Racer* bounced and lurched, and Addie started to panic.

"Space rocks," said Space Surfer. "Don't worry. We're almost there."

Addie held on to her seat. She tried not to focus on how fast everything was flying past. Outside her window space rocks, smaller galaxies, and constellations all whizzed by. *Space Surfer was right,* thought Addie. *The trip here was too quick! I want to see more.*

The *Racer* began to slow down and Addie could see a planet coming into view. It looked very purple.

"Check your mission packs," said Space Surfer. "There are wire cutters and a few other items you might need inside them."

Addie took a look inside her mission pack. "What are these other things?"

"Just clip it around your waist," said Valentina.

Addie put the mission pack on.

She quickly plugged her SpaceBerry into the remote control for the big screen.

A file came up on the screen.

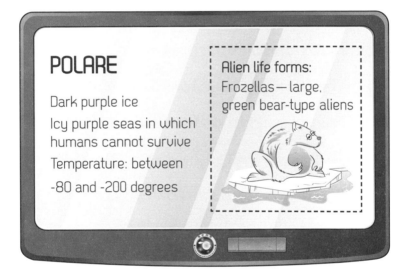

POLARE

Dark purple ice

Icy purple seas in which humans cannot survive

Temperature: between -80 and -200 degrees

Alien life forms:
Frozellas—large, green bear-type aliens

"Not bad," said Valentina. "Don't be fooled by those Frozellas, though. They might look kind of cute, but they are strong and very, very mean. Grab your ice poles. We need to take the pod down now."

Addie grabbed her poles and followed Valentina into the pod. It was a small spacecraft with two seats, a dashboard, and a hatch.

Space Surfer's voice came through the pod's speakers. "The pod is on autopilot and will land itself," he said. "I'll be waiting here with the *Racer.* You have an hour. After that your suits won't protect you from the cold as much. Good luck, Star Girl and Supernova 1." The pod hatch closed automatically and it took off toward Planet Polare.

As they got closer, the girls could see tall mountains of dark purple. At the foot of the mountains was purple ice.

This really is a frozen planet, thought Addie. *How can anything live here?*

"Look at that sea," Addie said to Valentina. "All the purple ice is sliding in, filling it." And that's when she saw the lime-green frozellas. There were three of them and they were stranded, floating on a small ice floe. "Valentina, they're stuck," said Addie. "We have to help them."

"No way," said Valentina. "That's not what we're here for. Anyway, they can swim."

"I read about them back at the FlyBy. They can't swim long distances. They're too heavy and their legs are made for walking more than swimming. And there are babies. It looks like a family."

Before Valentina knew what was happening, Addie had hit the autopilot override button. "Drive the pod down to them," said Addie. "I'll use the pod rope and ice pick to jump down onto the ice floe and ram the pick into the ice. The other end is attached to the pod, so you can pull us to shore."

"Are you crazy?" said Valentina.

"You can't go near those things. And we don't have time for this."

But Addie was already opening the hatch. She held the ice pick and rope in her hand, and she was getting ready to jump. *I'd better land on the ice floe*, thought Addie. *Humans can't survive in that cold, purple sea.*

She waited until the pod was directly above the ice floe. She took a deep breath.

One, two, three . . . Jump!

CHAPTER ★ FOUR

Addie landed right on the edge of the ice floe. She stumbled and nearly fell into the purple water. *Phew,* she thought. *That was a little too close.* Then the frozellas made a strange sound. The big one turned to look at Addie. It bared its teeth, and Addie's tummy did those familiar backflips. *I'd better hurry up and do this,* she thought.

Ramming the ice pick into the floe, she waved up at the pod. Then she heard a terrible noise.

Grrrroooooowwl!

"Please, I'm trying to help," she said to the frozellas, feeling pretty stupid.

Why am I talking to them? They can't understand me, she thought. But Addie kept talking just the same. It seemed to make her feel better. "You're such a cute little frozella cub," she said to one of the babies. It bared its teeth and growled. "Look, land," she said and pointed.

Addie jumped off the ice floe as soon as it hit the shore. She ran to where the pod had landed on the purple ice. Valentina was standing beside it with Addie's poles.

"They're safe!" said Addie.

"For now . . . but not for much longer. Look up," Valentina said.

Addie turned and saw a tall mountain of dark purple ice. It was quickly melting. Purple ice and liquid rushed down the side of it. "What's that black thing up on top of the mountain?" she asked. "And what's that noise?"

BRRRRR BANG BRRRRR

"I don't know, but I bet it has something to do with the ice melts," answered Valentina. She gave Addie her poles. "Activate the ice holds on your boots. We'll need them to climb up the mountain."

Addie activated her boots and long spike treads shot out from the soles.

Addie and Valentina began to climb.

"The noise is getting louder," yelled Valentina. She was in front of Addie and climbing fast.

BRRRRR BANG BRRRRR

"It sounds like a drill," said Addie. Just then an enormous hunk of melting ice flew down at them. "Watch out!" yelled Addie, and she hit the max-attach button on her poles.

Valentina looked up, but it was too late. The ice hit her and sent her flying. She slid and bounced past Addie on her padded bottom.

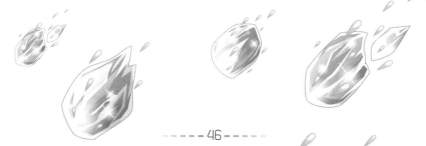

When Valentina finally stopped sliding and lay flat on her back, her broken poles continued to slide right down the mountain.

"Stay there," yelled Addie. "I'm coming down. Are you hurt?"

"I'm okay," Valentina called back. "Mr. Cruise was right. The extra padding really does help. And the space helmet protected my head. But my poles are broken. And gone! You keep going. I'll go back to the pod and wait. We don't have a lot of time left."

"No," said Addie, "we're supposed to stay together."

She slowly made her way to where Valentina was. She helped her up and checked her boots.

"At least your boots are still on the ice holds," said Addie. "Here, take one of my poles. We'll climb together."

"It's freezing," said Valentina, who had icicles hanging from her spacesuit. "We need to keep moving to stay warm. Even with wearing these suits."

They climbed slowly back up the mountain. Ice fell and purple water gushed down under their feet. The higher they climbed, the louder the noise became.

When they reached the top, they were exhausted. They both sat down on the flat plateau of hard ice and looked around.

"What is this place?" asked Valentina as she took out her SpaceBerry. "I'm going to get some pictures."

At the edge of the plateau was a tall pole with a massive dish on it. It looked like a satellite dish except that it was facing the ground instead of the sky.

Bright blue light shot out from the dish and shined down the mountain. It was melting the ice. In the center of the plateau was the big black thing they'd seen from down below. It was like a long pipe going down into the middle of the mountain.

Every sixty seconds it drove down into the mountain. Up close, the noise was really loud, and when the pipe moved, everything shook. Then it all went quiet and still until the pipe moved again.

"I wonder what the pipe does," said Addie.

"I wonder who put it and that dish that's melting everything here," said Valentina.

"I think we should use our holographic watches to call for help," Addie said. She went to flip the watch cover open but Valentina stopped her.

"We can do this mission ourselves," said Valentina. "I don't want help. We'll score more points if we do it ourselves."

"We've already used up forty-five minutes,"

said Addie. "In another fifteen minutes our suits won't protect us from the cold."

"All we have to do is stop that dish and then report in," Valentina insisted.

"How?" asked Addie. "And what about the black pipe thing? We don't even know what it's doing. I'm contacting Mr. Cruise."

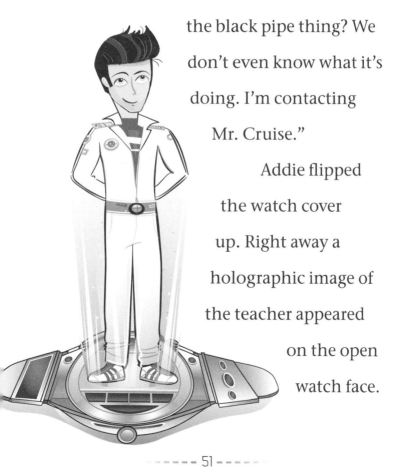

Addie flipped the watch cover up. Right away a holographic image of the teacher appeared on the open watch face.

"Star Girl, where is Supernova 1?" asked Mr. Cruise.

"She's sitting over there on the ice," said Addie. "We found what's melting the ice. And there's something else here too. Look." Addie moved her arm slowly in a circle so that Mr. Cruise could see the dish, the black pipe, and the melting ice.

"Good work, Star Girl," said Mr. Cruise. "Is there anyone else around? Any other alien life forms?"

"Not here," said Addie. "Just this machinery that seems to work by itself."

"Good. You need to stop the pipe. Its vibration must be cracking the ice and causing big ice sheets to break off and fall into the sea," said Mr. Cruise. "And you have to turn the dish off. The blue light is melting the ice at the same time."

"But how do we do it?" asked Addie.

"One of you must stop the pipe first to stop the shaking," said Mr. Cruise. "Find the power source. There will be two wires feeding the pipe. Cut the blue wire only. The other cadet needs to climb the ladder onto the dish. Somewhere up there will be a power box. In your mission pack is a magnetic disabler unit. Attach the MDU to the power box and it will do the rest. I'll have Space Surfer call the pod back to the *Galactic Racer*. Then he can hover over the plateau and pick you up from there." Then Mr. Cruise was gone.

Addie opened her mission pack and found the MDU. Valentina ran around the pipe and found the wires. "I'll do this," said Valentina. "The dish is yours."

Addie looked at the dish. It was so high up. And it was huge. Addie's hands began to sweat. She felt dizzy just looking at it.

CHAPTER ★ FIVE

"Off you go," said Valentina with a smirk. "You're the ballerina. The dish will be easy for you. I'll cut the wire on the pipe."

"You do gymnastics," said Addie. "You have much better balance than me."

"Afraid of heights, new girl?"

"No," said Addie in a voice that was just a little too quiet. *And I thought we were starting to be friends. Wrong!*

Addie began to climb the ladder. *Don't look down*, she thought. *Keep looking up.*

The ladder shook each time the pipe went down into the mountain. Addie held on tight. When she reached the top she was level with the dish. It curved in front of her like an upturned bowl. *The power box is on the other side,* thought Addie. *Right at the edge. I'll slide off the dish for sure.*

Then she remembered her space boots. "Valentina?" she called. "My poles are down there. Turn the ice holds off."

"Okay," Valentina called back. "I'll switch them to non-slip."

"And cut the wire on the pipe," Addie yelled. "I'm stepping out onto the dish now."

"Doing it right now," Valentina shouted back. But she didn't. She waited.

Let's see how good her balance really is, thought Valentina. *I'll give her just a little shake-up and then I'll cut the wire.*

Addie stepped out onto the dish. She walked across it quickly and carefully. The MDU was in her hand. *Nearly there,* Addie thought.

Suddenly the pipe began to move again.

BRRRRR BANG BRRRRR BANG BRRRRR

Everything started to shake. Addie bent down to attach the MDU to the power box. As she placed the MDU on the box, the dish shook so much that her non-slip boots couldn't save her. She dropped from the dish and landed right at the edge of the mountain.

Addie rolled and bounced on her big, padded bottom down the mountain. Valentina raced over to the edge of the plateau and watched. For a brief moment she thought she was going to laugh. The sight of Addie bouncing along did look funny, but Valentina knew this was bad. Suddenly she felt scared. Very scared. Then with one big bounce, Addie vanished from view.

Oh no! thought Valentina. *Where did she go?*

Taking out her SpaceBerry, she hit the radio button. "Supernova 1 to Space Surfer. Do you read me?"

A voice came out of the SpaceBerry.

"I read you, Supernova 1. What's wrong?" said Space Surfer.

"Star Girl fell and rolled down the mountain." Valentina knew she was shouting, but she couldn't help it. "I don't know where she is. I can't see her anymore!"

"Supernova 1, stay calm. I'm almost there," said Space Surfer. "I'll get you and we'll find Star Girl using the GPS tracking chip. Over and out."

Valentina put a hand inside her spacesuit. She felt her shirt pocket. There was the little hard square—the chip. Then Valentina felt really sick. *Seemed like a good plan at the time,* she thought. She raced over to the pipe and cut the blue wire. Everything went quiet and still.

★ ★ ★

Addie didn't know where she was. All she knew was that her arm hurt and she was shivering. Really shivering.

She lifted her head and looked down. She was on a steep patch of ice. It went straight down to the purple sea. The sea she knew she couldn't survive in. And that was when she saw them. Lime-green frozellas. And they were coming toward her.

No fast moves, thought Addie. *I don't want to slide into that sea. But I don't want to be dinner for a bunch of frozellas either. I'll get Mr. Cruise on holograph. Why am I soooo cold?*

Addie slowly moved to flip open her watch cover. "It's broken!" she said to herself. "Now what?"

The watch cover was smashed. The digital numbers had stopped, and the time had gone past one hour. *No wonder I'm shivering,* thought Addie. *The spacesuit isn't protecting me against the cold anymore.* Then she heard her SpaceBerry.

"Space Surfer to Star Girl, do you read me?"

It's Space Surfer, she thought. But she was so cold. She was getting sleepy and the frozellas were getting closer.

Addie managed to slide her SpaceBerry from the pocket of her spacesuit. She hit the button and spoke. "St-St-Star Girl to Spa-aace Surfer. I'm so, so, c-c-cold. Too t-t-tired. Frozellas. H-h-help."

The cold took hold and Addie fell asleep. The SpaceBerry slipped from her hands and onto the ice.

"Space Surfer to Star Girl," said Space Surfer. "I can find you using the SpaceBerry signal. Hang in there."

⋅⋆⋅⋆⋆⋅⋆⋆⋅⋆⋅

The lights of the *Racer* woke Addie. The first thing she noticed was that she was warmer. *They've rescued me,* she thought. Then she saw the *Racer* up above her. The ice was hard under her back. *No. I'm still here,* Addie thought. *But I'm as warm as toast. How?*

Addie carefully lifted her head. She was

confused and didn't know where she was. The last thing she remembered was feeling super cold and very sleepy. And now she was warm. She looked around her. *I'm surrounded by frozellas,* she thought. *They're cuddling around me and keeping me warm and safe.*

"Now I remember," she said aloud as she wrapped her arms around the baby. "I was on a steep piece of ice and was too scared to move. You must have come and rescued me. But how?"

The baby just cuddled into her neck. "If only you could talk, little guy," she said. "I'd love to know how you got me from that steep ice and onto this flat ice. But who cares, really. I'm just so glad to see furry green things like you. My beautiful little family from the ice floe."

Above Addie, a spacestretcher was being lowered from the *Racer* down to the ice. Space Surfer was sitting in it.

"Time to go, Star Girl," said Space Surfer. "Can you stand?"

Addie stood up very slowly. The mother frozella sat in front of her, making sure she didn't topple into the sea.

"I think I'm all right," she said. "I hurt my arm and leg, though."

"Let's get you onto this stretcher," said Space Surfer. "As soon as we have you back on board we can get you some first aid."

"Wait," said Addie, and she turned to her furry family. "Thank you, guys!" she said. "You saved my life. You're not mean at all. I wish I had a photo of this to show everyone back at SEAS."

"No problem, Space Girl," Space Surfer said as he lifted his SpaceBerry up. "Say cheese!"

Addie stood in between her little frozella family and smiled.

"Got it," said Space Surfer. "Now it's really time to leave. In the space stretcher you go!"

CHAPTER ★ SIX

Valentina was sitting in her seat on the *Racer* when Addie and Space Surfer returned.

"I'm so glad you're all right," Valentina said. "I was so scared! What happened?"

"One minute I was on the dish and the next I was rolling down the mountain," Addie said. "I don't really remember, though. I just remember flying through the air and landing somewhere else."

"You can take your suits and helmets off now," said Space Surfer. Then he handed Addie a space blanket. "Wrap yourself in this and then both of you fasten your seat belts. We're out of here in two minutes."

The girls removed their helmets and Space Surfer locked them into the *Racer's* helmet hold. Valentina unzipped her spacesuit and bent down to unlock her boots. As she did, the tracking chip fell from her shirt pocket. She quickly stood on it with her boot. But she wasn't quick enough. Addie and Space Surfer saw it.

They looked at each other but Addie said nothing. Valentina held her breath and looked at Addie. Addie turned away.

★ ★ ★ ★ ★

Mr. Cruise was waiting for them in the FlyBy when they returned.

"What happened out there, girls?" he asked. "Space Surfer told me about the fall. Did you cut the pipe wire first, like I said?"

Valentina jumped in before Addie had a chance to speak. "The wire was cut, Mr. Cruise," she said. "Addie fell from the dish. It curved down pretty steeply." Addie noticed that Valentina elected not to say exactly when the wire was cut.

"Where's your tracker chip, Star Girl?" asked Mr. Cruise. "You know very well it's against the rules to remove it or turn it off."

Addie stared at the ground. She could feel Space Surfer's eyes on her. She looked at Valentina. She was staring at Space Surfer.

"Well?" asked Mr. Cruise.

"I'm not really sure," said Addie. "I just know that my watch is completely broken. I must have hit it hard on the ice out there, I guess."

"Do you have anything to add about this, Supernova 1?" asked Mr. Cruise.

"No, Mr. Cruise," said Valentina as she shifted on her feet.

"Well, the important thing is that you are all right, Star Girl. Just a few bruises," said Mr. Cruise. "You both did a good job out there. We've already sent a team in to take the machinery apart and remove it. Polare and its frozellas are safe now. Good work. You'll score extra points for saving that family on the floe, too."

"Yes!" said Valentina.

"But we will have to deduct points from both of you because of the chip. We lost your signal the moment you left the FlyBy, Star Girl. So you didn't lose it out there on the ice. Are you sure you have nothing more to say on the subject?"

Addie remained quiet. She simply shook her head.

"All right then," said Mr. Cruise. "Back to your dorm rooms now. And don't forget to do your mission reports. I will be reading them very carefully."

Back in the dorm room, Addie sat down at her computer. She was about to start her report when Valentina came over and sat down beside her. "You're not so bad after all, new girl," she said. "I sent a space mail to Mrs. Lamrock. I said that I was okay with getting a new roommate. I asked Miya's roomie if she wanted to swap rooms. She said yes. She's a neat freak like me. We get along well." Valentina smiled.

"I'll get to share with Miya?" asked Addie.

"Yep. You'll make a good space cadet, Addie," said Valentina as she left the dorm room.

I guess that's Valentina's way of saying sorry, Addie thought. *But hey, sharing a room with Miya! Awesome!*

Just then SpaceChat flashed open on Addie's computer. It was Space Surfer.

SPACE SURFER

Hey Star Girl, How are you doing?

STAR GIRL

I'm good now. Valentina agreed to a room change. I get to share with Miya 😊

SPACE SURFER

That's great! Hey, here's the picture I took on my SpaceBerry.

STAR GIRL

Great pic! Thanks, SS. 🧸

SPACE SURFER

So, are you going to say something about the tracker chip in your report?

STAR GIRL

Nah . . . It's done now. I can tell she feels really, really bad. And actually, I think we're kinda friends now.

SPACE SURFER

You think? I dunno. It's all about cadet scores with her. Are you going to Beach Island this weekend?

STAR GIRL

I hope so. That place sounds totally amazing. I can't wait to see inside. Miya says the rapid rides in there are awesome.

SPACE SURFER

I might see you there then. Watch out for yourself, Star Girl. CYA.

STAR GIRL

CYA 🙂

SEAS HEAD OFFICE:

Your mission scores

Adelaide Banks: 7 points.
Points deducted: 3 (new tally: 4)

Valentina Adams: 7 points.
Points deducted: 3 (new tally: 38)

New ranking: 2.

TOP TEN SPACE CADET SCOREBOARD

NAME	PHOTO	CADET POINTS	HOUSE
Grace Mauro (SC Comet XS)		40	NEBULA
Valentina Adams (SC Supernova 1)		38	NEBULA
Louisa Jeffries (SC Star Cluster)		37	NOVA
Aziza Van De Walt (SC Asteroid)		35	NOVA
Hannah Merrington (SC Galactic 6)		34	METEOR
Miyako Wakuda (SC Astron Girl)		29	NOVA
Lara Walsh (SC Red Giant)		28	METEOR
Sabrina Simcic (SC Neuron Star)		26	NEBULA
Olivia Marston (SC Orbital 2)		24	STELLAR
Molly Lopez (SC White Dwarf)		12	STELLAR

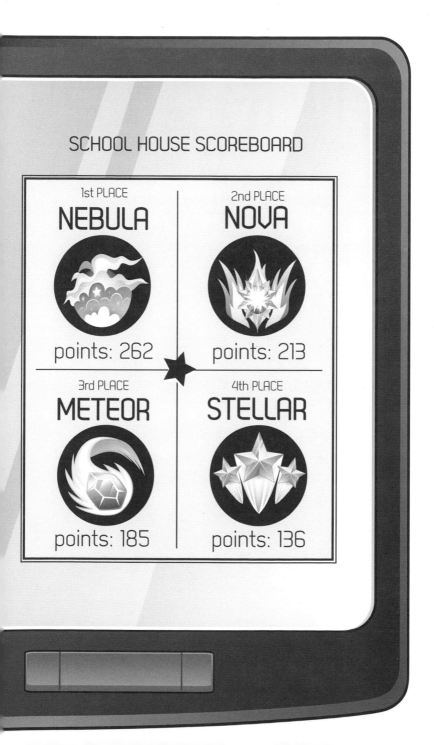

Check out all of Star Girl's space adventures!